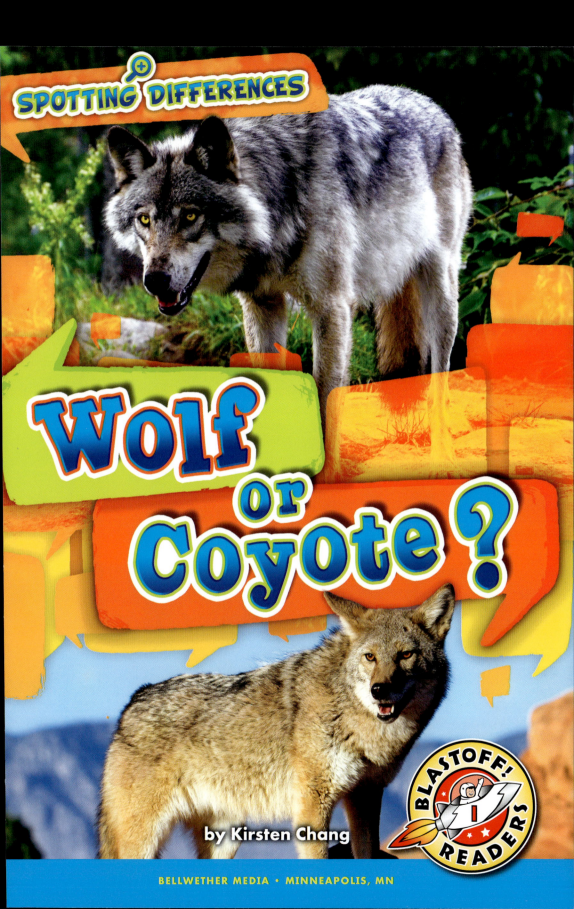

Note to Librarians, Teachers, and Parents:

Blastoff! Readers are carefully developed by literacy experts and combine standards-based content with developmentally appropriate text.

Level 1 provides the most support through repetition of high-frequency words, light text, predictable sentence patterns, and strong visual support.

Level 2 offers early readers a bit more challenge through varied simple sentences, increased text load, and less repetition of high-frequency words.

Level 3 advances early-fluent readers toward fluency through increased text and concept load, less reliance on visuals, longer sentences, and more literary language.

Level 4 builds reading stamina by providing more text per page, increased use of punctuation, greater variation in sentence patterns, and increasingly challenging vocabulary.

Level 5 encourages children to move from "learning to read" to "reading to learn" by providing even more text, varied writing styles, and less familiar topics.

Whichever book is right for your reader, Blastoff! Readers are the perfect books to build confidence and encourage a love of reading that will last a lifetime!

This edition first published in 2020 by Bellwether Media, Inc.

No part of this publication may be reproduced in whole or in part without written permission of the publisher. For information regarding permission, write to Bellwether Media, Inc., Attention: Permissions Department, 6012 Blue Circle Drive, Minnetonka, MN 55343.

Library of Congress Cataloging-in-Publication Data

Names: Chang, Kirsten, 1991- author.
Title: Wolf or Coyote? / by Kirsten Chang.
Description: Minneapolis, MN : Bellwether Media, Inc., 2020. | Series: Blastoff! Readers: Spotting Differences | Includes bibliographical references and index. | Audience: Age 5-8. | Audience: K to Grade 3.
Identifiers: LCCN 2018058080 (print) | LCCN 2018059265 (ebook) | ISBN 9781618915788 (ebook) | ISBN 9781644870372 (hardcover : alk. paper)
Subjects: LCSH: Wolves--Juvenile literature. | Coyote--Juvenile literature.
Classification: LCC QL737.C22 (ebook) | LCC QL737.C22 C415 2020 (print) | DDC 599.773--dc23
LC record available at https://lccn.loc.gov/2018058080

Text copyright © 2020 by Bellwether Media, Inc. BLASTOFF! READERS and associated logos are trademarks and/or registered trademarks of Bellwether Media, Inc. SCHOLASTIC, CHILDREN'S PRESS, and associated logos are trademarks and/or registered trademarks of Scholastic Inc., 557 Broadway, New York, NY 10012.

Editor: Al Albertson   Designer: Jeffrey Kollock

Printed in the United States of America, North Mankato, MN.

Table of Contents

Wolves and Coyotes	4
Different Looks	8
Different Lives	14
Side by Side	20
Glossary	22
To Learn More	23
Index	24

Wolves and Coyotes

Wolves and coyotes are **mammals** with thick fur. They are **similar** to dogs.

coyotes

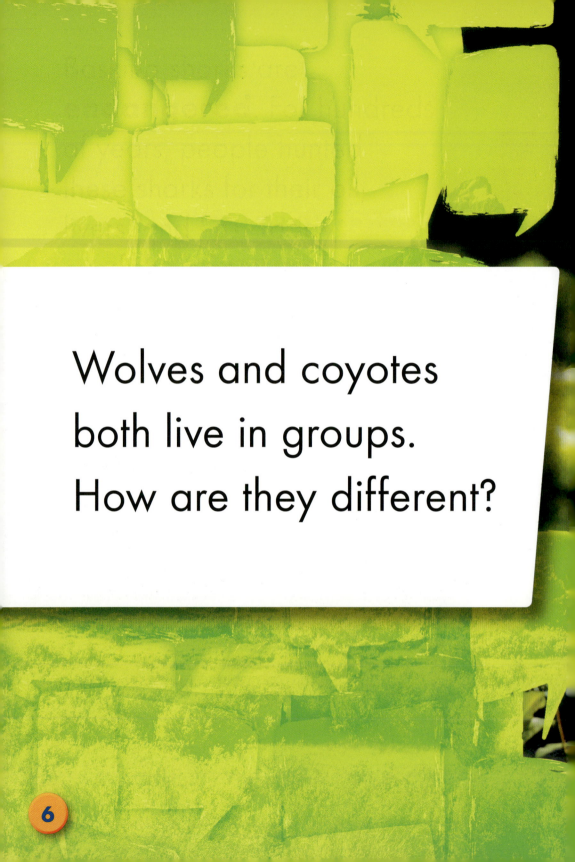

Wolves and coyotes both live in groups. How are they different?

wolves

Different Looks

Wolves are big.
They have wide **snouts**.
Their ears are short.

snout

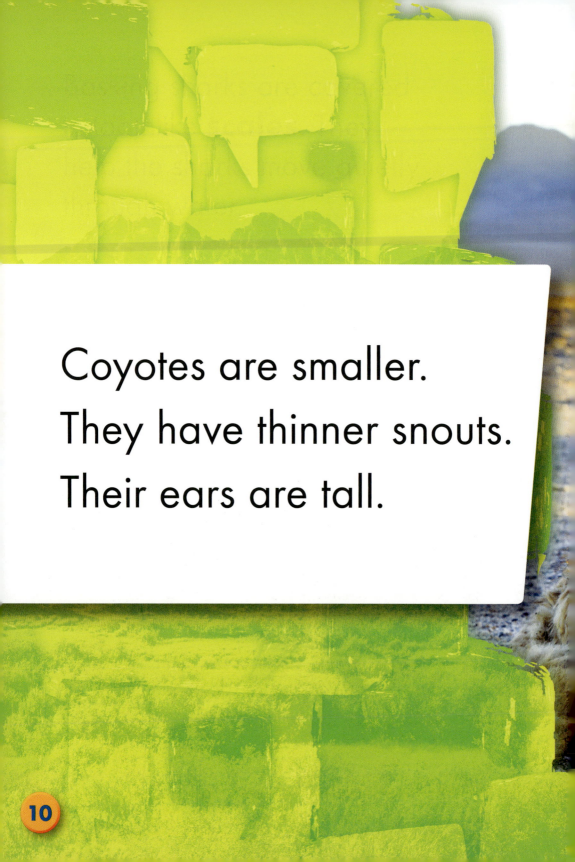

Coyotes are smaller.
They have thinner snouts.
Their ears are tall.

Wolves can be gray, black, or white.
Coyotes are often gray. Some are red and brown.

Different Lives

Wolves and coyotes make sounds to **communicate**. Wolves **howl** a long, low call.

howling

Coyotes bark. The sound is short and **high-pitched**. They howl, too.

barking

Wolves hunt large animals like elk. Coyotes hunt small animals like rabbits. Which hunter is this?

Side by Side

gray, white, or black fur

short ears

wide snout

Wolf Differences

howl to communicate

hunt big animals

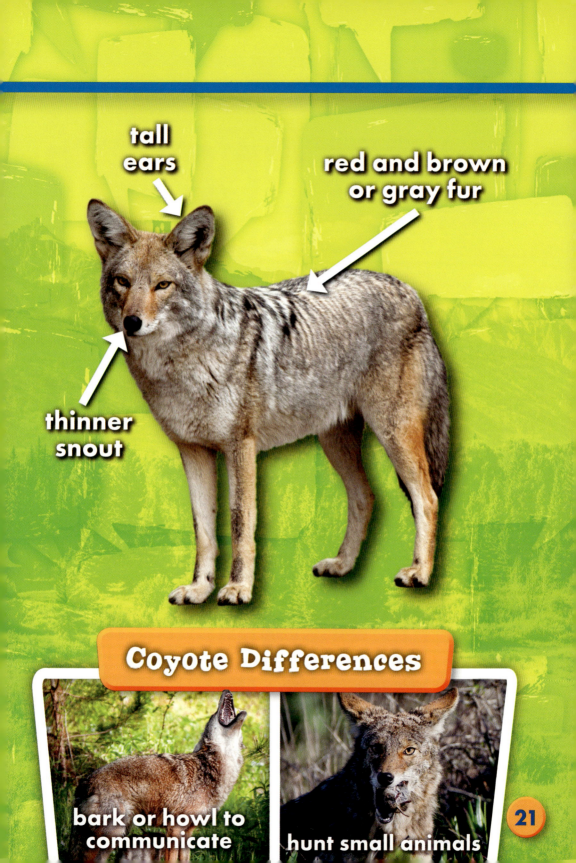

Glossary

communicate

to share information or feelings

mammals
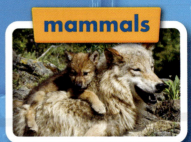
warm-blooded animals that have hair and feed their young milk

high-pitched

higher in sound

similar

close to the same

howl

to make a long, loud noise

snouts

the noses of some animals

To Learn More

AT THE LIBRARY

Gagne, Tammy. *Coyotes*. Lake Elmo, Minn.: Focus Readers, 2017.

Grack, Rachel. *Wolves*. Mankato, Minn.: Amicus Ink, 2019.

Hansen, Grace. *Coyotes*. Minneapolis, Minn.: Abdo Kids, 2016.

ON THE WEB

Factsurfer.com gives you a safe, fun way to find more information.

1. Go to www.factsurfer.com.

2. Enter "wolf or coyote" into the search box and click 🔍.

3. Select your book cover to see a list of related web sites.

Index

animals, 18
bark, 16, 17
communicate, 14
dogs, 4
ears, 8, 10
fur, 4
groups, 6
howl, 14, 15, 16
hunt, 18
mammals, 4
snouts, 8, 9, 10
sounds, 14, 16

The images in this book are reproduced through the courtesy of: David Boutin, front cover (wolf); Warren Metcalf, front cover (coyote); Derek R. Audette, pp. 4-5, 6-7; Chris Alcock, pp. 8-9; dmodlin01, 10-11; AndreAnita, pp. 12-13; FRAYN, p. 13 (bubble); Stayer, pp. 14-15; Warren Metcalf, pp. 16-17; Richard Mittleman/Gon2Foto/ Alamy, pp. 18-19; Jim Cumming, p. 20 (wolf); Bildagentur Zoonar GmbH, p. 20 (howl); Geoffrey Kuchera, p. 20 (hunt); Fabio Michele Capelli, p. 21 (coyote); Holly Kuchera, pp. 21 (bark), 22 (snouts); Matt Knoth, p. 21 (hunt); karl umbriaco, p. 22 (communicate); wavebreakmedia, p. 22 (high-pitched); Red Squirrel, p. 22 (howl); Vibe Images, p. 22 (mammals); Eudyptula, p. 22 (similar).